Terr
Tina

Written and illustrated by
Nick Ward

OXFORD
UNIVERSITY PRESS

OXFORD
UNIVERSITY PRESS

Great Clarendon Street, Oxford, OX2 6DP,
United Kingdom

Oxford University Press is a department of the University of Oxford.
It furthers the University's objective of excellence in research, scholarship,
and education by publishing worldwide. Oxford is a registered trade mark of
Oxford University Press in the UK and in certain other countries

Text and Illustrations © Nick Ward 2017

The moral rights of the author have been asserted

First published 2017

British Library Cataloguing in Publication Data
Data available

978-0-19-837763-4

5 7 9 10 8 6 4

Paper used in the production of this book is a natural, recyclable product
made from wood grown in sustainable forests. The manufacturing process
conforms to the environmental regulations of the country of origin.

Printed in China by Golden Cup

Acknowledgements
Inside cover notes written by Gill Howell

Contents

Chapter 1
Double Trouble!

There's no doubt that Tina can be naughty. She talks with her mouth full, wipes her nose on her sleeve and loves playing tricks on people. She puts glue on door handles and salt in sugar bowls, and people can often be heard muttering, "Oh Tina, that's a terrible thing to do." Which is how she got her nickname: Terrible Tina!

Head Teacher

Tina's teacher, Miss Brick, wasn't perfect either. Sometimes she got very grumpy and shouted. And she was always sucking liquorice, which made her teeth go black. Miss Brick didn't let anyone else suck sweets in class, and Tina thought that was very unfair. So she decided to have some fun.

One day, during breaktime, Tina crept into her classroom and put a big, fat slug in the liquorice bag on Miss Brick's desk (I said she was naughty!). When everyone filed back into class, Tina sat at her table and waited. Miss Brick didn't notice anything unusual until the piece of liquorice she was about to pop between her lips started to wriggle, and two little antennae popped up in surprise!

"Pah!" Miss Brick quickly put the slug down and glared at Tina.

Tina cackled in delight.

Miss Brick wasn't happy. "Tina, that's a terrible thing to do."

7

Miss Brick wiped her lips with a tissue. She knew Tina must be to blame. "If you've got time to play tricks, you can't have enough work to do. Go and tidy the stationery cupboard."

"Oh, but *Miss*," complained Tina. She hated tidying the stationery cupboard, which wasn't really a cupboard at all. It was a small, cobwebby room filled with books, pens, glue, paper and lost property. It smelled of pencil shavings and old socks.

"No arguments," said Miss Brick.

Grumpily, Tina went to the stationery cupboard. It was in a terrible mess. The shelves were groaning under the weight of pads, markers and text books. A big box of crayons had spilled all over the floor and Tina began to pick them up.

"This isn't fair!" muttered Tina. "There are hundreds of crayons!" It wasn't long before she became bored.

Absentmindedly, Tina started to doodle on a large piece of paper stuck to the wall. With a fistful of different colours, she could make a whole rainbow with just one sweep of her arm, or make multicoloured waves. She drew a picture of Miss Brick swimming amongst the waves, and added a ferocious shark chasing her! It was only then that she realized she'd been scribbling on Miss Brick's timetable chart.

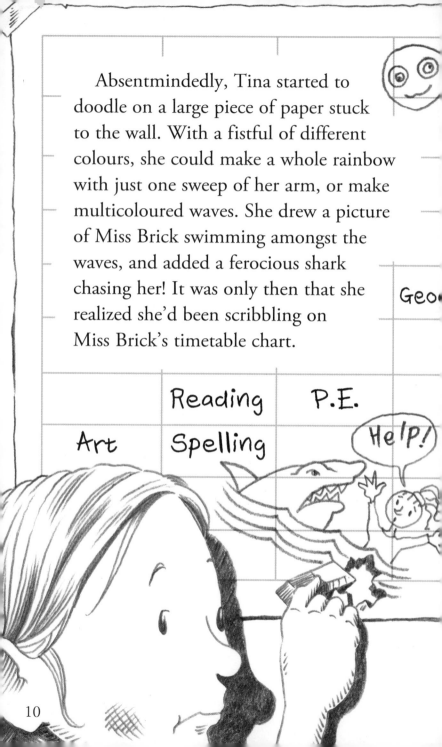

Geo

Reading   P.E.

Art   Spelling   Help!

"Uh-oh!" gasped Tina, knowing she would be in real trouble if Miss Brick found out. She looked around for an eraser and found one in a box of paper clips. She rubbed furiously at her drawings but the eraser was old and hard, and it made a nasty hole in the chart. Tina started to panic. Then she saw the old photocopier that Miss Brick used to copy their worksheets.

"That might do it," thought Tina, although she wasn't quite sure how it worked. "If I copy the chart on to a new piece of paper, it won't have a hole in it."

Maths   P.E.

Tina was here!   Citizenship

Tina had been told many times never to touch the photocopier, but she was in a desperate situation. She pulled a chair over to the machine, climbed up and lifted the lid. "I think this goes here," she thought, placing the chart on the glass. "And then I press this button."

It was then that things started to go wrong. Tina pressed the start button but as she did so, the chart began to slip off the photocopier. She made a grab for it, lost her footing and fell on to the machine, just as its light flashed and its motor whirred.

Tina was blinded for a minute, and squeezed her eyes shut. When she opened them, she was astounded to see an exact copy of herself standing in front of her. True, the copy was as flat as a piece of paper and her colour was a bit faded, but other than that she was just like Tina!

13

"It's gone very quiet in there," Miss Brick suddenly called out. "Are you still tidying up, Tina?"

"Yes, Miss Brick," said Tina and her copy at the same time, and they both burst into a fit of giggles.

"Well it doesn't sound like it. Finish what you are doing and then come and rejoin the class."

Chapter 2
Tina Two Has All
the Answers

"You go," said Terrible Tina to her copy.

"No!" said Tina Two.

"It'll be fun!" insisted Terrible Tina.
When her double still wouldn't go,
Terrible Tina gave her a shove. Miss Brick
was busy writing on the whiteboard, so
she didn't see Tina Two stumble into
the classroom. But she heard the excited
whispers and giggles of the rest of the class
when they saw Tina Two.

"Are you playing the fool, Tina?"
asked Miss Brick. She spun around and
saw Tina Two.

"Oh, my word," Miss Brick thought. "She's as thin as a piece of paper, and so pale. Perhaps I've been working her too hard!"

"Are you feeling all right, Tina?" asked Miss Brick with a nervous grin.

"Yes, thank you, Miss Brick," said Tina Two.

"Well come and sit down, dear," said Miss Brick, fussing around the paper-thin girl and trying to sound especially friendly. Oh dear! What would the head teacher say if she found out a student had been nearly worn away by overwork? Miss Brick decided she would have to be much nicer to the naughtiest girl in the class.

"How about a nice cushion for that hard chair?" Miss Brick asked.

"Yes please," said Tina Two, and Miss Brick gave Tina Two the special, embroidered cushion from her own chair. The rest of the class looked very confused.

What was going on?

Back in the stationery cupboard,
Terrible Tina was becoming confused
too. She had been peering through a gap
in the door and chuckling to herself,
watching Miss Brick get in a flap.
What was even better was that Terrible
Tina had found Miss Brick's supply of
liquorice sweets, and she was already on
her third one. Now, though, Miss Brick
was being extra nice to the new Tina.
This was unheard of!

"It's not fair!" muttered Terrible Tina. She'd been looking forward to somebody other than herself getting into trouble, even if it was her exact copy. Now that copy was being waited on hand and foot. First, the teacher gave Tina Two the cushion, then she asked if she was warm enough and turned on a little fan heater. Finally, Miss Brick asked if the paper girl was hungry, and gave her an iced bun out of her own lunchbox. It was incredible!

If Terrible Tina thought things were bad, though, they were about to get a whole lot worse.

"As it's getting near the end of term, we're going to have a little quiz to find out how much you remember from your lessons," Miss Brick announced.

"Ugh!" groaned the class, but Tina Two looked quite content.

"Now she'll be in trouble," thought Terrible Tina. "She won't know anything and Miss Brick will stop being so nice."

Tina Two, though, was very, very clever! When Tina's image went around the insides of the photocopier, something had happened. It had picked up all of the information from Miss Brick's worksheets that had gone through the photocopier in the past. Tina Two knew all the answers to Miss Brick's questions without even having to think about them.

"What is forty-seven plus eight?" asked Miss Brick.

In the stationery cupboard, Terrible Tina started to count on her fingers.

"Fifty-five," said Tina Two, almost
before Miss Brick had finished talking.

"Well done," said Miss Brick, a little surprised. The other children looked at Tina Two suspiciously. Miss Brick tried a harder question.

"What is three quarters of twenty-four?" she asked.

"Eighteen," cried Tina Two, her hand shooting into the air.

"Very good, Tina," said the teacher, beaming at her new star pupil. "Now we'll have a history question. What can anyone remember about the first man on the moon?"

"Oh, I know," thought Terrible Tina in the cupboard. "He got sick from eating too much moon cheese!"

Tina Two's hand shot up again. "The first man on the moon was Neil Armstrong," she said, like a paper robot. "His rocket was called Apollo Eleven and it landed in the Sea of Tranquility, which isn't really a sea at all but a large flat plain, on the twenty-first of July in 1969."

"Y-y-yes," stammered Miss Brick. She was very impressed. "What a remarkable change," she thought. "Tina's like a completely different girl!"

$\frac{24}{4} \times 3 =$

The first man on the moon was...

Terrible Tina was definitely not impressed. "What a goody two shoes," she muttered to herself. She could see the amazed looks of all her school friends, and knew her role as class joker was in danger. It was time to shake things up a little!

Chapter 3
Terrible Tina
Has a Plan

As the quiz continued and Tina Two carried on answering all the questions, the real Tina crouched behind the cupboard door. She cupped her hands together and blew gently between her thumbs. It made a spooky, hooting noise.

"Woooh!" No one took any notice. Terrible Tina blew harder. "Wooooooh!"

"What's that?" asked Emily Watson, who was sitting nearest to the stationery cupboard. She looked nervously around the classroom. "Did anyone hear it?"

Woooooh!

"Wooooooh!" Terrible Tina warbled
again and the class went very quiet.
"It's working," she thought. She slowly
opened the door to an old metal locker
that stood next to her. The rusty hinges
squealed mournfully.

Eeeaaaooowwweee!

"It's a ghost!" said Jimmy Jones in the back row, his eyes as big as saucers.

"A ghost!" gasped Miss Brick, going very pale. "Good grief, surely not?"

Terrible Tina nearly burst out laughing, but then Tina Two jumped out of her chair and marched over to the stationery cupboard.

"Don't worry, Miss. It's just an annoying draught," she said, closing the door with a clunk. She knew exactly what Terrible Tina was up to!

"I don't believe it! Foiled by my own copy," thought Terrible Tina. She had just been about to pour a box of paperclips on to the floor, hoping they would sound like the rattling of ghostly chains. She had other plans but she wouldn't be able to carry those out until lunchtime, when everyone was out of the way. Now she would have to wait among the spiders and the cobwebs in the dark.

It seemed a very, very long time until the bell sounded for lunch, but Terrible Tina had plenty to do. Despite the darkness, she managed to creep silently around the stationery cupboard, knocking spiders off their webs into an empty chalk box. When she had caught about twenty spiders, she carefully closed the lid.

"Hee, hee, hee," she giggled quietly. "Someone's going to get a spider surprise!"

Finally, Terrible Tina heard the muffled voices of her classmates as they filed out for lunch. She waited a moment, opened the cupboard door a fraction and put her eye up to the gap. The classroom was empty, so she tiptoed over to the whiteboard. With a whiteboard pen, she drew a very big picture of her teacher eating a huge slug. Pleased with her work, she drew another one of Miss Brick with wide, staring eyes and wild hair shouting, "It's a ghost!" She finished by signing it 'Silly Miss Brick, by Tina'.

"That will really get goody two shoes Tina Two into trouble!" she said with a grin.

Terrible Tina opened the little round pot on Miss Brick's desk where she kept her erasers and clips and elastic bands, and emptied all the spiders from her chalk box into it. Miss Brick was always dipping her hand into the pot for something or other. Next time she would get a horrible, hairy shock!

Terrible Tina hurried over to the classroom wormery. This was a tall glass tank filled with layers of mud, sand and stones. Inside the mud lived hundreds of worms, and you could see all the little tunnels they made as they moved around inside. Terrible Tina took off the lid, pushed her hand inside and pulled out a handful of muddy, wriggling worms. Yuk!

She rinsed them under the tap at the sink in the corner then quickly put one in each of her friends' pencil cases. She could just picture their faces when they took a pencil out for the afternoon spelling lesson, only to find it wriggled and writhed and crawled across the table!

Suddenly, Terrible Tina heard a noise in the corridor outside and made a dash for her hiding place. She had just managed to shut the door when Tina Two marched into the classroom. The rest of the class couldn't be far behind.

"This is going to be fun!" chuckled Terrible Tina to herself.

Chapter 4
Terrible Tina's Plan Goes Wrong!

But it wasn't fun. Tina Two spoiled everything! She seemed to know exactly what Terrible Tina had been up to.

"It's as if she can read my mind," thought Terrible Tina, as Tina Two hurried around the classroom, collecting all the worms from the children's pencil cases and putting them back in the wormery. Perhaps she *could* read her mind – she was Tina's copy, after all!

Next, Tina Two straightened all the chairs in the classroom, found a jar for a bunch of buttercups she'd picked in the playground and put it on Miss Brick's desk. She noticed the stationery cupboard door was standing ajar and, with a sly grin, she opened the pot on Miss Brick's desk and shook all the spiders into her hand. Then, walking calmly over to the cupboard, she threw the spiders through the gap and ran off.

"Yikes!" cried Terrible Tina as the spiders landed in her hair, crawled across her face and dropped down the front of her jumper. They wriggled and tickled and scuttled about. "Just you wait!" she yelled, and she was about to rush out of the cupboard when Miss Brick and the rest of the class came in.

Tina Two was standing right next to the whiteboard. It still had Terrible Tina's drawings on it. All Miss Brick had to do was turn her head and she would see them!

"She won't be able to get out of this one," thought Terrible Tina, but as Miss Brick turned to face the board, Tina Two knocked a box of drawing pins off the desk.

"Sorry, Miss," said Tina Two as the pins were scattered across the floor.

"Never mind," said Miss Brick, with a forced smile. She crouched down and started to pick them up. "Everyone, stay where you are or you might stand on them," she said.

As Miss Brick was picking up the pins, Tina Two had time to wipe the board clean.

"There we are. No harm done," said Miss Brick, standing up and putting the box back on her desk. Then she saw the tidy classroom, the clean whiteboard and the little bunch of flowers. "Who has tidied the classroom?" she asked.

"I did, Miss," said Tina Two.

"Thank you, Tina. It looks lovely," said Miss Brick. She was amazed. Tina was usually the untidiest girl in the school. Miss Brick took two gold stars and stuck them next to Tina's name on the star chart. They were the first stars Terrible Tina had ever been given!

"Thank you, Miss," said Tina Two.

"You deserve it," said Miss Brick.

Watching from the stationery cupboard, Terrible Tina snorted. It seemed her double could do no wrong. Now she was a proper teacher's pet. How on earth would Terrible Tina live it down – and how on earth was she going to get rid of her interfering photocopy?

Chapter 5
Terrible Tina Gets Locked Out

After that, Terrible Tina's afternoon got even worse. Miss Brick was so impressed with Tina Two that she cancelled the spelling lesson and let everyone read or paint or play instead. Tina Two was suddenly very popular with the whole class!

As the children played quietly, Miss Brick and Tina Two sat and chatted like old friends. Tina Two told stories and facts and jokes, and Miss Brick laughed and clapped. "This girl's a phenomenon!" she thought.

Trapped in her hidey-hole, Terrible Tina groaned. "That girl is a pest," she thought. "And if I don't want to spend the rest of my life living in this cupboard, she'll have to go." The tricky part, though, was how to get rid of Tina Two.

Everything Terrible Tina had tried so
far had resulted in Tina Two looking even
better in Miss Brick's eyes. She would
have to bide her time and wait for an
opportunity.

Unfortunately, the opportunity never came. When Terrible Tina's mum came to pick her up, Miss Brick ran over with Tina Two.

"I just had to come and tell you what a remarkable daughter you have, Mrs Payne," she said. "Quite brilliant."

Tina's mum looked very surprised. "Are you sure?" she asked. Then, looking at the paper girl she added, "Are you all right, Tina?"

"I'm fine," said Tina Two.

"She does look a little pale, but I've put that down to studying too hard," explained Miss Brick. "She seems to know the answer to everything!"

Mrs Payne wasn't convinced. "You look different somehow, Tina," she said. "Let's get you home."

"Different? She's made of paper!" muttered Terrible Tina to herself. She'd crept outside and was peering around the corner of the school building to where her mum stood with all the other parents. Perhaps she should just march across the playground and own up to her prank. But she might get into all sorts of trouble.

"Bye, Miss Brick. See you tomorrow," said Tina Two as Tina's mum led her out of the playground and down the road. Terrible Tina followed at a safe distance. She'd always fancied being a spy or a private detective, and now she could put her spy skills to the test.

She followed Mum and Tina Two along the High Street, ducking behind lamp posts whenever Tina Two looked over her shoulder. When they went into the supermarket, Terrible Tina was not far behind. She followed them up and down the aisles, watching in astonishment as her mum filled a trolley with all her favourite foods – fish fingers, chicken drumsticks and peas; cake, jelly and ice cream.

"You look as if you need feeding up," said Mrs Payne, giving Tina Two a kiss on the cheek. "So, I'm going to cook you your best tea ever!"

"Thanks," said Tina Two, like a
little robot.

"Not fair!" Terrible Tina fumed from behind a tower of soup cans. Everyone seemed to prefer this new Tina, and she didn't like it. What's more, Tina Two was getting a special tea and Terrible Tina was really, really hungry. Her tummy rumbled and gurgled as she followed her mum and her double out of the shop and all the way home.

Her mum opened their front door and left it ajar as she took the heavy shopping through to the kitchen. Terrible Tina tried to slip in behind them, but Tina Two saw her and slammed the door in her face. Now she was shut out of her own house! Angrier than ever, Terrible Tina crept around to her back garden and peered through the sitting room window. Tina Two was already sitting at the coffee table, doing her homework. What a goody two shoes she was. She hadn't even asked to watch the television first!

47

Terrible Tina knocked on the window. "You're for it," she mouthed silently, in case her mum heard her. Tina Two smiled, jumped down from her chair, marched over to the window and closed the curtains.

Terrible Tina stamped her foot and folded her arms and scowled. Things weren't going well, and now it was starting to rain!

"Oh, that's just brilliant," she said and stomped around to the kitchen window.

Chapter 6
Bath Time!

The rain was coming down fast now, and Terrible Tina was soaking wet. She could see her mum cooking fish fingers and chicken drumsticks through the steamed-up glass. When her mum opened the window to let out some steam, the most wonderful smells wafted out, making Tina hungrier than ever.

"This is torture," she moaned, peeping over the windowsill and starting to shiver as little rivulets of water trickled down her face.

Terrible Tina watched Mum put ketchup and pickles and a glass of frothy milkshake on the table. Then she dished up a big plateful of chips, peas, chicken and fish fingers.

"Tea's ready, Tina," Mum called, and Terrible Tina was so cold, miserable and hungry, she ran towards the back door that led into the kitchen. She'd already started to turn the handle when she remembered her mum wasn't talking to her!

"Thank you," said Tina Two, coming in from the front room and sitting at the kitchen table.

"Ooh!" whimpered Terrible Tina in despair.

"What was that noise?" asked Mum.

"Just a mangy old moggy who can smell the fish fingers, I expect," said Tina Two with a knowing smile.

"Well, tuck in then," said Mum, and Tina Two started to nibble at a chip.

People made of paper don't have much of an appetite, though, and Tina Two had soon eaten enough.

"But you've hardly touched your food," said Mum when Tina Two asked to get down. "Now I know you're not very well."

"I'm OK, Mum. Really," said Tina Two.

"I'm not so sure," said Mum. "I'll run you a nice warm bath and then it's straight to bed. If you're not better in the morning, I'm taking you to the doctor's."

Tina Two followed Mum out of the kitchen and up the stairs. At last, Terrible Tina could open the back door and get out of the rain. She dried her hair as best she could on a tea towel, stuffed a fish finger into her mouth and followed her double upstairs. The stairs squeaked and creaked, and Terrible Tina stopped and held her breath. Had she been heard?

No, the noise had been hidden by the sound of water filling the bath. *Phew!*

Terrible Tina breathed out again and sneaked along the landing. She peered through the open doorway, into the bathroom.

"In you get then," said Mum as her head disappeared inside the airing cupboard. "I'll find you an extra-soft, extra-warm towel."

Now, paper people can't take their clothes off, as the clothes and the person are all the same piece of paper. So Tina Two just stepped straight into the bath and sat down. Then, as Terrible Tina watched her copy cover herself in soapy bubbles, a very strange thing happened. Tina Two started to fall apart. (Well, she was only paper, after all!)

First, her colours began to run. Then her paper body became soggy and turned into a lumpy mush, like porridge. Soon, all that was left of Tina Two was a thin, grey film floating on top of the water. Terrible Tina couldn't believe her eyes. Or her luck! She stepped into the bathroom just as her mum pulled a towel from the airing cupboard and turned around.

"Here we are," she began, and then stopped. She looked at Tina and then at the bath.

"Just a minute," she continued, feeling very confused. "I thought you were already ... Oh, never mind. Hurry up and get in before the water gets cold."

55

Terrible Tina slipped out of her clothes and jumped into the bath. As her mum took some clean pyjamas through to her bedroom, Tina gathered up all the paper mush, wrung it out and dropped it into the wastepaper basket.

"Just where it belongs," she said to herself with a grin. She wrapped herself in the warm, soft towel and went to her bedroom. Her mum was folding clothes and putting them away.

"Well, you look much more like your old self," said her mum. "You were looking very poorly."

"Oh, I'm fine now, Mum," replied Tina with a grin.

Once she was in her pyjamas and dressing gown, she went downstairs and finished the special tea that Tina Two had left. It was delicious, and Mum was so pleased Tina was feeling better, she let her have two helpings of ice cream for dessert. With chocolate sauce!

Chapter 7
Terrible Tina is Back in Charge!

Now, I'd like to say that Terrible Tina had learned some sort of lesson from her antics, and that she became as good as gold overnight. She'd seen how popular Tina Two had been with Miss Brick and her school friends. Even her mum had treated Tina Two to a special tea, so you'd expect Terrible Tina to change her ways, wouldn't you? Well, she tried very hard to be a little less naughty, but she wasn't always successful.

Just the very next day, she put sticky tape under the mouthpiece of Harry Connor's trumpet! When Harry tried to play the trumpet in assembly, nothing happened. He huffed and puffed until his cheeks were as big as balloons and his face as red as a tomato, but the sticky tape made the trumpet impossible to blow. All he produced was an awful screech and a loud raspberry! The school hall rocked with laughter, and Terrible Tina could feel Miss Brick's disapproving eyes boring into the back of her head.

But Miss Brick didn't say anything. She was so relieved to see Terrible Tina looking her old self again, she was being much nicer to her. This made Terrible Tina much nicer to Miss Brick in return. She tried to keep quiet during lessons, and helped by handing out worksheets. She kept all the classroom pencils sharp, and never went near the photocopier again! Miss Brick was so pleased that she gave Terrible Tina another gold star.

But Tina was still terrible and she couldn't go for long without playing tricks. During a painting lesson, Terrible Tina broke off a small piece from a tablet of red watercolour paint. She'd noticed the filter cap on the end of classroom tap could be unscrewed. Pretending to wash her hands, she took the cap off, put the pellet of paint inside and replaced the cap. When Miss Brick turned the tap on, the water came pouring out bright red.

61

"Oh my word, it's blood!" Miss Brick shrieked. She came over all faint and one of the children had to help her to a chair and fan her with a book. She soon realized it was a trick, though, and she stared hard at Tina. Terrible Tina was pretending she hadn't noticed anything. She was innocently painting a picture of a pretty flower, and trying very hard not to grin.

The best trick, though, happened just today. Terrible Tina brought a warty old toad into class and put it in Miss Brick's lunchbox. Miss Brick thought it was her apple and went to take a huge bite out of it. You could hear her scream from the other side of the school!

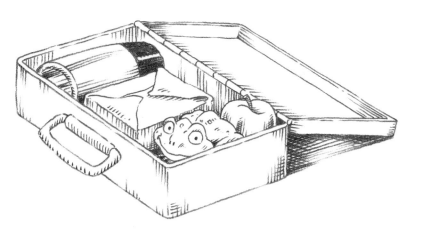

"Terrible Tina! Come here!" she yelled.

About the author

When I was little and saw a photocopier for the first time, my dad told me it would copy anything you put on the glass top. I wanted to put a bar of chocolate on it, and make lots of bars chocolate which I could eat. No such luck. All it did was make a picture of a bar of chocolate!

As I began writing this story, I wondered what would happen if a copier could make a walking, talking copy of a real, live person. What fun that would be!